# MARY-KATE & ASHLEY

## Starring in

# HOLIDAY IN THE SUN™

A novelization by Eliza Willard

Based on the teleplay by
David T. Wagner and Brent Goldberg

HarperEntertainment
*An Imprint of HarperCollinsPublishers*

A PARACHUTE PRESS BOOK

**PARACHUTE PRESS**

Parachute Publishing, L.L.C.
156 Fifth Avenue
New York, NY 10010

 DUALSTAR PUBLICATIONS

Dualstar Publications
c/o Thorne and Company
1801 Century Park East
Los Angeles, CA 90067

### ☚HarperEntertainment

*An Imprint of* HarperCollins*Publishers*
10 East 53rd Street, New York, NY 10022.

Book created and produced by Parachute Publishing, L.L.C., in cooperation with
Dualstar Publications, a division of Dualstar Entertainment Group, Inc., published by
HarperEntertainment, an imprint of HarperCollins Publishers.

For information address HarperCollins Publishers Inc.,
10 East 53rd Street, New York, NY 10022.

ISBN 0-06-106668-0

HarperCollins®, ☚®, and HarperEntertainment™ are trademarks of
HarperCollins Publishers Inc.

First printing: November 2001

Printed in the United States of America

## mary-kateandashley.com
### America Online Keyword: mary-kateandashley

Visit HarperEntertainment on the World Wide Web at
www.harpercollins.com

10 9 8 7 6 5 4 3 2 1

# CHAPTER ONE

"Ah, Hawaii," Madison Stewart said as she lounged on the deck of a yacht. Surrounded by ten cute guys, Madison took a long, slow sip of her pineapple smoothie.

She gazed across the turquoise water toward the sandy beach. There, she saw her twin sister, Alex. Alex was leaning back on a towel, surrounded by ten cute boys of her own.

"Looking good, Alex!" Madison called to her.

"*Feeling* good, Madison!" Alex called back.

Madison closed her blue eyes and took in the sea air. "What could be cooler than a vacation in Hawaii?" she wondered dreamily. She opened her eyes to gaze at the beach once more. But instead she saw...her science teacher standing in front of a chalkboard. What was Mr. Vaughn doing here?

"And where does oxygen come from?" Mr. Vaughn was saying. "The carbon dioxide or the hydrogen dioxide? Anyone? Anyone?"

Madison's shoulders slumped. It was all a daydream. She wasn't in Hawaii. She was in Washington—in science class!

She turned to her sister, Alex, who was sitting one desk away and wearing a dreamy grin. "Alex," she whispered.

"Huh?" Alex snapped back to reality.

"Were you dreaming what I was dreaming?" Madison asked.

"Winter break in Hawaii," Alex whispered, "with an army of cute boys?"

"You got it!" Madison said. She gripped her sister's hand in excitement. It was the last day of school before winter break—and their high school class was going on a trip to the Hawaiian Islands!

"It's going to be so awesome," Madison whispered. "Our first chance at independence. We're going to have the time of our lives!"

Madison and Alex were fifteen years old. They weren't little girls anymore. They were pretty blond teenagers who were almost old enough to drive. But their parents didn't get it yet. Sometimes they still treated them as if they were kids.

This winter break everything would change. The trip to Hawaii would be their first trip without their mom and dad. And Madison was totally psyched!

"Which flip-flops should I bring?" Alex asked.

"The hot-pink, electric-blue, or the red ones with the plastic daisies?"

"All of them," Madison whispered back. "You can never have too many flip-flops."

*Ding!* The speaker above the classroom door sounded. "Alex and Madison Stewart," a voice announced. "Please report to the principal's office."

Madison stared at Alex. Why did the principal want to see them? What did they do?

"Go," Mr. Vaughn told the girls.

Alex and Madison stuffed their books into their backpacks. As they walked up the aisle to the door, they could hear some students mumbling.

They left the classroom and walked through the hall. Madison's head was spinning. "Did you return those overdue library books?" she asked.

"I thought *you* did!" Alex wailed.

Madison stopped short. She spotted a woman standing in front of the principal's office. The woman was wearing funky black glasses and a business suit. "That's Katherine," Madison said, surprised.

Katherine was their father's assistant. But what was she doing at school?

"What's wrong?" Madison asked her. "Is it dad?"

Their dad, Harrison Stewart, was the head of a major investment company. His job took him on business trips all over the world. This latest trip has been a really long one—one month and counting! They weren't sure when he was coming home.

"Your dad's fine," Katherine said. "But he did ask me to pick you up from school early. You're finished with all your finals, right?"

"Right," Alex and Madison said together.

"And you aced them?" Katherine asked.

The girls looked at each other. "Hopefully!"

Katherine flashed a mysterious smile. "Then let's get going."

Madison and Alex grabbed their winter jackets from their lockers and followed Katherine out of the school. They all stepped into a waiting black limousine.

The chauffeur drove them straight to the airport. Madison's heart beat faster as the limo pulled up to a shiny private jet waiting on the runway.

"It must be pretty important," Alex said as they hurried toward the jet.

"Very," Katherine said. She stopped at the bottom of the steps that led to the plane's door. Then she gave a little wave. "Bon voyage!"

Confused, the girls waved back and climbed aboard the plane. They looked around, even more confused. Where were the other passengers? Or the flight attendants with the honey roasted peanuts?

"Welcome aboard!" a man's voice boomed.

Alex and Madison spun around. The door to the pilot's area was open. And smiling at the controls was...

"Dad!" Madison cried happily.

Harrison Stewart stepped out of the pilot compartment. Madison was happy to see her dad but she didn't get it. Instead of his usual business suit, he was wearing khaki shorts and a polo shirt—in the middle of winter!

"Buckle up," he said. "We'll be cleared for take-off soon."

"Where are we going?" Alex asked excitedly. "Hawaii?"

"I know!" Madison jumped up and down. "You're flying us there early so we can get a head start on our tans!"

"Oh, this is much better than Hawaii," Dad said with a sly smile. "We're going to Atlantis."

Madison stopped jumping. "Atlantis?" she asked slowly. "You mean...the lost continent? The one that sunk in the ocean?"

"No." Dad laughed. "The resort in the Bahamas."

The Bahamas? Madison couldn't believe it. "But we wanted to go on our school trip to Hawaii," she said. "We don't have any friends in the Bahamas."

"And there aren't any luaus in the Bahamas," Alex added.

"Or hot lifeguards," Madison said. She shook her head and blushed. "I mean...what's there to do in the Bahamas anyway?"

"You can hang with me and your mom," Dad answered.

Madison began to panic. What about their independence? This was supposed to be their first trip *without* their parents.

Alex gulped. "But—" she began.

"Look," Dad said. "I've been gone for a month. I've had meetings all over the world and now I need my family. And a beach. And a few of those goofy drinks with the paper umbrellas."

"But what about mom?" Alex asked. "Where is she?"

"Your mom doesn't like company jets so she flew ahead," Harrison explained. He swept his hand to the row of seats. "So have a seat, girls. We're out of here!" Dad slammed the airplane's door closed.

Madison sighed as she and Alex walked slowly to their seats. *This is it,* she thought glumly. *There's no way out. We're stuck on another family vacation.*

# CHAPTER TWO

*It's beautiful,* Alex thought as the plane swooped over Paradise Island, Bahamas. She stared at the blue water, snowy white sand, and leafy green palm trees. But Alex couldn't help it. She still wanted to be in Hawaii with her friends.

The plane landed on the tarmac near a white limousine. As the girls descended the stairs they could see Judy Stewart stepping out of the car.

"Mom!" the girls called as they ran over.

"What do you think?" Judy asked.

"This place looks so pretty!" Madison said, hugging her mother.

"But we were hoping we could go on vacation on our own," Alex admitted. "Even if it was with our teacher and friends."

"And at least we'd have the right clothes," Madison said. She slung her heavy ski jacket over her shoulder.

"Your summer clothes are hanging in your hotel closet," Mom said. "I took care of all that."

Harrison walked over and kissed Judy on the cheek. "How was your flight?" he asked.

"Smooth," Judy replied.

"Did the Graysons get here in one piece?" Harrison asked.

"Don't know," Judy answered. "We can check when we get to the hotel."

*The Graysons?* Alex said to herself. *Again?* "Dad, why do we have to vacation with the Graysons every year?" she moaned.

"Because Chad Grayson is my business partner. And good friend," Harrison said with a smile.

"Well, Alex and I just took a vote," Madison said.

"We did?" Alex asked.

"Yup. A silent one," Madison replied. "Dad, we decided you need more friends."

Dad laughed. "Well, I'll keep the ones I have, but thanks for the advice."

"Come on, girls," Judy said. "You *have* to see the hotel. It's a blast!"

They all piled into the limousine. When they arrived at Atlantis, Alex gasped. Mom was right. The grounds were awesome!

The hotel was surrounded by bright tropical flowers and lush plants. Waterfalls cascaded over sparkling swimming pools. A huge aquarium was filled with lobsters, neon-colored fish, coral, and sea plants. Steps away from the hotel was the turquoise-colored ocean and a sugar-white beach.

"This place is fantastic!" Madison said as they stepped into the hotel lobby. It was filled with white wicker furniture and even more tropical flowers.

They walked across the polished marble floor. A bellhop in uniform followed the Stewarts with their luggage on a rolling cart.

"How many rooms did we get, Mom?" Alex asked even though she knew the answer. She and Madison would be sharing a room with their parents as usual.

Judy Stewart smiled excitedly at her husband.

"We have a surprise for you," Harrison said.

Mom nodded. "You two worked very hard in school this year. So I think it's time you had your own suite!" She reached into her straw bag and pulled out two keys.

Alex was speechless. She and Madison took their keys and hugged their parents. Maybe their mom and dad were finally treating them like grown-ups. Maybe this vacation wouldn't be so bad after all!

"Now, why don't you two check the front desk to see if the Graysons have made it in yet," Harrison suggested.

"Our own suite!" Madison squealed as they walked over to the marble desk. "That's practically our own apartment!"

But just as the girls reached the desk, a girl with long, dark hair stepped directly in front of them. She wore a white bikini and a floral sarong wrapped around her tanned waist. There was a flashy gold chain bracelet around her wrist and one around her ankle too.

"Hey!" Madison complained.

The girl glanced back but didn't budge. "Oh," she said. "Were you in line?"

Alex and Madison opened their mouths to speak. The girl flipped her hair over her shoulder and turned back to the desk.

"Brianna Wallace," she told the woman who was working there. "Messages for my father, please."

"Who does she think she is?" Alex whispered to Madison.

The woman behind the desk smiled eagerly at Brianna. Her nametag read LIZ. "Certainly, Miss Wallace," Liz said. "And how is your father?"

"He's in the casino," Brianna replied. "Probably wondering why this is taking so long."

The woman grabbed a wad of pink messages. "Sorry," she said. "Of course, I—"

Brianna snatched the message slips. "Thank you." She turned around and caught Madison and Alex staring at her. "And thank *you*," she said, and walked away.

"How rude," Alex said. "Next time—take a number!" she called after the girl.

"Forget her," Madison muttered. She stepped up to the desk and smiled at Liz. "Excuse me. Have the Graysons checked in?"

Judy and Harrison joined the girls just as Liz checked her computer screen. "Sorry," Liz said. "They're not here yet."

"Oh, yes, we are!" a cheery voice shouted.

The Stewarts whirled around. The Grayson family was crossing the lobby.

Chad Grayson was about the same age as Harrison. He was wearing tan pants and a T-shirt. His wife, Jill, was an attractive woman with a bright smile. She was dressed in a yellow sundress and sandals.

Then there were the kids—Griffen and Keegan. Griffen was seventeen and always a bit nerdy. But Alex had to admit his new wire-rimmed glasses looked cool on him.

Standing next to Griffen was eight-year-old Keegan. She wore her hair in pigtails and had freckles on her nose. She also had a monster IQ, and never let anyone forget it.

The parents greeted each other with hugs.

"Hi, everybody," Alex and Madison chimed in.

Alex watched as Griffen's eyes darted directly to Madison. She always knew that he had a little crush on her sister. She even told Madison about it once, but Madison didn't believe her.

"Hi, Madison," Griffen said.

Keegan cleared her throat. *"And—"*

Griffen blushed as he turned to Alex. "And Alex," he added.

"Hi, Griffen," Alex said with a grin. "What's up?"

Before Griffen could answer, their parents were already planning their day. But Chad wanted to talk about business.

"Chad," Harrison said with mock seriousness. "As your CEO and friend, I direct you to put all business aside for the next five days."

"It's difficult," Chad said.

*He really needs to loosen up,* Alex said to herself. Her thoughts were interrupted by a soft rushing noise. "Hey, I can hear the ocean!" she said.

Madison tilted her head to listen. "Yeah! And it's calling our names!"

● ● ●

In a flash the girls were in their swimsuits and on the beach. Madison wore a denim bikini and red board shorts. Alex wore a blue two-piece with matching sunglasses.

"The Bahamas are great and everything," Alex said as they shared a table near the beach. "But we're old enough to be on our own now. I mean— we're turning eighteen."

Madison rolled her eyes. "What?"

"In three years," Alex added. Then she spotted a cute guy wearing orange swim trunks. He was carrying a surfboard under his arm. Alex nodded toward him. "There's a good one, Madison."

Madison lowered her sunglasses to look. "Not bad," she said.

A waiter strolled by carrying a tray of tropical fruits and juices.

Alex grabbed a coconut drink for herself and a strawberry drink for Madison. Then Alex took a sip of her drink and relaxed into her chair. When she thought about it, she knew she and Madison were lucky to be there. How many kids got to go to Paradise Island? "I just wish we could have a little freedom this year," she told Madison.

"How hard could that be?" Madison replied. "We'll just plan a lot of stuff to do. If we have a lot of stuff planned, then Mom and Dad can't make plans for us." She took a sip of her strawberry drink. "And we have our own room, right? That means they can't check up on us twenty-four seven."

Alex smiled. "You know what, Madison? I think this place is really growing on me." She sucked down the last drop of her fruit drink. Then she heard the sound of engines revving up.

"Check it out!" Madison said.

Alex followed Madison's gaze. Tearing across the ocean were people on shiny Sea-Doos!

"I feel the need..." Madison declared.

"The need...for speed," Alex added. "Come on, Madison, let's go!"


Griffen gazed at the ocean from a lounge chair on the beach. He could see Madison riding an electric blue Sea-Doo. Her blond hair flew as she and her sister raced over the waves.

*Madison*, Griffen thought. *She's so pretty, so smart, so cool....*

"I know who you're looking at," Keegan's voice sang.

"Shut up, runt!" Griffen snapped. "Don't sneak up on me like that. And I wasn't watching Madison. I was scanning the horizon for...for ships!"

"Right." Keegan sighed. "That's why 'I like Madison' is written all over your face."

Griffen rolled his eyes. "Give me a break," he muttered. "What do you know?"

"Everything," Keegan said. "I have an IQ of one sixty, remember?" She crossed her arms and studied her brother. "Do you know what the saddest words in the history of the universe are?"

"That we have to share a hotel room again?" Griffen joked.

"Very funny," Keegan said. "The saddest words are 'what might have been.' As in, why didn't I do what I really wanted to do." She pointed at Madison and gave her brother a nudge. "Make your move!"

Griffen watched as Keegan skipped back to the pool. How did she know he liked Madison, and that he was too shy to do anything about it?

He turned back to the beach. He spotted Madison right away. She and Alex were riding toward the shore now. Madison caught Griffen staring and waved at him.

Griffen gave a tiny, embarrassed wave back. Maybe his little sister was right. Maybe he *should* make his move.

# CHAPTER THREE

"That was awesome!" Madison cried as they steered their Sea-Doos toward the shore.

"Okay, I've made a decision," Alex told Madison as they waited to return their Sea-Doos. "I'm officially letting go of the whole Hawaiian vacation thing with our friends. It's gone....Well, maybe not *gone* gone, but I'm trying really hard to work through it."

"A strong move," Madison said. She was startled when a hand reached out and grabbed the handle of her Sea-Doo. She glanced up and saw a white-haired man with piercing blue eyes.

"Oh, hi," Madison said with a smile, but he didn't smile back. "We're just returning these."

"Good. Get off," the man replied.

Alex and Madison hopped off their Sea-Doos. The man gave Alex's Sea-Doo to another customer and dragged Madison's away.

Madison shook her head. "There's a guy who really hates his job."

The girls began walking along the beach.

Madison spotted a boy who was high above the ocean in a parachute. He was attached to a cord and was being pulled by a speedboat. Even from a distance Madison could tell he was really cute.

"Look!" Madison pointed at the boy parasailing.

"That looks like fun," Alex said.

The parasailer landed neatly on the sand. He brushed back his thick brown hair. Then he stepped out of his parachute and walked toward the girls.

"Impressive," Madison said with a smile.

"Thanks." The boy flashed a smile back at Madison. Then he pulled a yellow flyer from his pocket and handed it to her.

" 'Yacht party,' " Madison read aloud. " 'Dance till whenever on the *Silver Star*. Slip 2010. Tell them Scott sent you.' " She looked up. "Are you Scott?" she asked the boy.

"Yup," he said. "Don't forget." He pointed to the yellow flyer. "Slip 2010."

"We'll be there," Alex replied as he walked away.

"Wow," Madison said. "He's hot."

"No kidding," Alex said. "The Bahamas keep getting better and better."

That evening, Madison, Alex, and their parents met the Graysons for dinner. They shared a large table overlooking the bay. Madison was waiting for the perfect moment to ask Dad if she and Alex could go to the party.

"So, how come you girls are all dressed up?" Judy Stewart asked Madison and Alex. She took a sip of her coffee.

Madison cringed. Now wasn't the moment. "Dressed up?" she said with a nervous grin. She smoothed her satiny sleeveless dress.

"We're not dressed up," Alex added, decked out in her cropped white pants and tiny silver tank top.

They had wanted to ask Dad earlier if they could go. But he kept talking about how much he missed them while he was away, and that he wanted to spend every second with them. Madison didn't have the heart to tell him that they had planned to go to a party.

Harrison smiled at his daughters. "They look so good, I wish I could take them to a party and show them off." He bopped Madison on the head with a hotel brochure he had picked up in the lobby earlier.

Madison slumped in her seat. She and Alex exchanged a look.

Dad opened the brochure. "It says here the Caribbean has always been a haven for smugglers and pirates." Harrison looked up from the brochure.

"Maybe they ought to beef up security here."

"Come on, Dad," Alex said. "We have nothing pirates want."

Keegan tugged at her necklace.

"Did you make that pretty necklace, Keegan?" Judy Stewart asked.

Madison studied the necklace. It looked like a bunch of tiny white shells strung together.

"Oh, it's nothing," Keegan said. "Just a typical string of molluskless cone habitations."

Everyone stared at Keegan.

"You know...puka shells," Keegan explained.

Jill Grayson stroked her daughter's hair. "It's a work of art, honey." She turned to Madison's mom. "Both of my children are gifted. You know, Griffen will be going to Yale next year."

"Any idea what you want to study, Griffen?" Madison asked.

"Well, I've always been interested in flying insects," Griffen began.

"Oh!" Madison said. "So you're going to study entomology!"

"No," Griffen said. "I'm thinking aeronautical engineering. I want to build things that fly."

"Cool!" Madison said, impressed. She could tell that Griffen was impressed with her too. After all, how many fifteen-year-olds knew entomology was the study of insects?

A waiter with white gloves delivered a silver tray to the table. On it was a piece of paper.

"Thanks," Harrison said. "Just what I've been waiting for." He took the paper and studied it. "Our concierge has made some great suggestions for fun this week. Hanging with the dolphins. Water slides… and that's just the daytime!" he added. "Tonight they're having a talent show out by the pool. I thought we could all sing a song together. You know, show 'em how talented the Stewart family is."

Madison glanced at Alex and cleared her throat. Now was the moment to tell Dad. Now or never. She didn't want to be stuck singing in a talent show when she could be dancing with Scott.

Alex spoke up first. "Um, yeah, Dad, it sounds great." She looked at her wrist. "Oh, wow, would you look at the time!" Alex exclaimed. But she wasn't wearing a watch.

Dad laughed. "Who cares what time it is? We're on vacation!"

*Okay. We definitely need a plan B,* Madison thought. *Maybe the direct approach.* "Dad, may we be excused?" she asked. "A boy from the beach invited us to a party."

"A party?" Judy repeated.

"I don't know," Harrison said. "Where is it?"

"Right here at the hotel," Alex said. "Slip 2010 at the marina. It's the yacht party of the season."

Madison held her breath while her parents exchanged looks. *Please let us go,* she thought.

"All right," Harrison finally said. "But you have to be back in your room no later than eleven."

"Yes!" the girls cheered.

"Dad, is it cool if I go too?" Griffen asked.

"Sure," Chad answered.

"Come on, you guys." Madison jumped up from her chair. "Let's go and find that Scott!"

All eyes turned to Madison. Her cheeks burned when she realized what she had said.

"I mean *yacht.*...Let's go find that yacht!"

*Wow,* Alex thought as she gazed up at the huge, elegant ship docked in the harbor. A rock band played while kids danced on deck. Waiters roamed the crowd, carrying trays of food.

Alex, Madison, and Griffen boarded the yacht and stepped onto the main deck.

"Do you believe this?" Madison asked Alex.

Alex shook her head, staring happily around her. The guys all seemed cute. And the girls were dressed really cool—in sleeveless dresses, tiny tank tops, and cropped pants.

"I'll get the drinks," Griffen offered.

"Pineapple smoothies for us," Madison said, her eyes darting around the deck. "Thanks a lot."

The band started playing a slow song. Alex looked to the stage. The lead singer strummed his guitar and sang. He had brown hair and big, dreamy brown eyes. He looked a little younger than the rest of the band, maybe sixteen, Alex thought.

She nudged Madison. "Yottie—twelve o'clock."

"Yottie?" Madison followed Alex's eyes to the stage but looked confused.

"A hottie on a yacht," Alex explained. "A yottie."

The singer caught Alex's eye. He smiled at her as he sang.

"He's smiling at you," Madison whispered.

"I saw that," Alex said, staring at the singer. Then he winked at her, and she realized he'd caught her staring. "And now he *knows* that I saw that," Alex said, turning red.

The band finished the song, and Alex clapped along with everyone else. Out of the corner of her eye, she noticed Scott, the cute parasailer from the beach, walking toward them.

He stopped in front of Madison. "Hey, uh, want

to dance?" he asked her with a grin.

"When there's some music," Madison replied.

"Oh, yeah, right," Scott said.

Alex stifled a giggle. *He must feel like a complete idiot*, she thought.

"I'll bet there's more music on a big boat like this," Madison told Scott. She took his hand. "Let's go find some."

*Way to take charge, Madison!* Alex thought as her sister walked away with Scott. Then she turned her attention to the stage. The musicians were setting down their instruments to take a break. The lead singer jumped off the stage and started walking in her direction.

*I don't believe it,* Alex thought. *He's headed straight for me. Stay cool, girl....* She glanced at the juice bar, trying to seem casual. She noticed Griffen at the back of a long line, waiting to be served.

"Hi. What's your name?" the singer asked.

"Alex," she replied, facing him.

"That's it? Just one name?"

"That's one more than you," Alex said.

He smiled. "Jordan. Are you here on vacation with the family?"

"Yeah. How about you?"

"I live here," Jordan said. "I work at Atlantis,

taking care of the fish," he explained.

*Atlantis?* Alex's heart beat faster. "Oh," she said, trying to sound calm. "That's where I'm staying."

As she talked to Jordan, Alex noticed a slight commotion on the deck. Three girls had just boarded the yacht. Alex recognized one of them— Brianna Wallace. The girl who had cut in front of her and Madison at the reservation desk.

Alex bit her lip as she watched them push through the crowd. A nice-looking boy spotted Brianna and smiled at her.

"Hi," he said.

"*Bye,*" she replied, walking right passed him.

*Typical,* Alex thought. Then she noticed that Brianna was staring right at Jordan.

"I'm fascinated by the stingrays," Jordan was saying. "They're one of my favorites."

"Aren't stingrays dangerous?" Alex asked.

"Excuse me," Brianna interrupted. She stepped between Alex and Jordan. "My name is Brianna Wallace, as in the Wallace Department Store Wallaces."

"Jordan Landers," Jordan told her. "As in the Landers Hardware Store Landerses."

Brianna smiled. "A sense of humor. Cute." She turned to Alex. "Sorry, I don't believe I know you."

"Sure you do," Alex replied. "Remember? Take a number?"

Brianna studied Alex. "Sorry. I don't remember ever seeing you." She flashed a mean grin. "But I guess you hear that a lot."

"Cute," Alex told Brianna.

"Hey, man, great set." Two guys and a girl surrounded Jordan, patting him on the back.

Brianna whisked Alex off to the side. "Now that we've met," she said. "I just want to get a few things straight. I always get what I want. And this winter break...I want Jordan." Then Brianna waltzed off, pulling Jordan away with her.

Alex stood there, shocked. She couldn't believe Brianna had the nerve to steal Jordan away like that. She didn't care if Brianna was used to getting her way. Alex liked Jordan too, and she wasn't going to back down.

"Brianna Wallace," she whispered. "Let the games begin."

# CHAPTER FOUR

"We have a message," Alex said as she and Madison entered their hotel suite later that night. "Who do you think called us?"

Madison picked up the phone and listened to the recording. She gulped. "That was Dad," she said, hanging up. "He wants us to call him the instant we come in."

*Knock. Knock. Knock.*

"Too late." Alex sighed. "He's here."

Madison held her breath as her sister opened the door. Their parents marched in.

"Good morning, girls," Harrison said. "I say *morning* because it is now twelve-fifteen A.M. How late does that make them, Judy?"

"One hour and fifteen minutes past curfew," Judy announced.

"But if we were back home we'd be one hour and forty-five minutes *early*," Alex said. "Right now in Washington it's *nine*-fifteen."

"Nice try, Alex," Madison said. She turned to her

mom and dad. "We're really sorry."

"Well, we had a great time tonight," Judy said. "And it would have been nice to share it with you."

*We had a great time tonight too,* Madison thought. *At least I did.* She felt warm and fuzzy when she remembered dancing with Scott in the yacht's lounge.

A couple of times she'd caught Griffen watching them. He didn't seem to be having such a great time. *He should have found a girl to dance with,* Madison thought, feeling a little bad for him.

"Just get to bed, girls," Harrison said. "We've got a full day tomorrow."

"But I've got a day date!" Madison blurted out.

"A day date?" Harrison asked.

"A date during the day," Madison explained. "I'm going horseback riding with Scott."

"Who's Scott?" Harrison narrowed his eyes.

"A beach hottie," Madison replied.

Harrison looked at his wife for help.

"A cute boy," Judy translated for him.

"And I was going to concentrate on chillin' by the pool," Alex told them.

"That's fine," Harrison said. "But you're both going to do your chillin' with us."

"But what about my day date?" Madison asked

as sweetly as she could. She really wanted to go.

Dad sighed. "We'll see…" he said.

"Okay," Madison said, but she already knew what the answer would be. *We'll see* always meant *no*.

"You sure are good with horses," Madison said the next day. She and Scott were riding side by side along a deserted stretch of beach. The waves lapped lazily onto the shore. It was beautiful and relaxing.

Dad had really surprised her that morning. As a compromise, he had said that she and Alex could go off on their own *if* they spent the entire morning with him and Mom. So, that morning they all hung out by the water slide. It had been kind of fun to play like kids again—for a while.

Hanging out with Scott was fun too. Madison just wished that he would *say* something to her. They'd been riding together for almost an hour— and they had exchanged only a few words! *Maybe I should ask Scott another question*, Madison decided. "Um, how did you learn to ride so well?"

"My uncle owns a ranch," Scott replied.

"Oh," Madison said. There was another long silence as they rode on.

"So…do you go there a lot?" she asked him. "To your uncle's ranch?"

"I guess," Scott said. That's all he said.

Madison could think of only one more question. Why wasn't he talking to her? *Maybe he's the strong, quiet type. Or maybe he has a sore throat. Or maybe...he doesn't like me,* Madison thought glumly.

"Whoa." Scott pulled on his horse's reigns.

"What's up?" Madison asked, slowing down too. "Why are we stopping?"

"No reason," Scott said. "Just felt like stopping."

*This is it,* Madison thought. *He's going to tell me he's bored and then say it was nice knowing you.*

But Scott just stared at the hazy horizon.

"Don't you have anything to say to me?" she asked him.

"Um. Sure." Scott said. "Race you back to the stables!" He bridled his horse and charged down the beach.

"Hey!" Madison raced after him. Soon her horse was galloping beside his, then passing it.

"No fair!" Scott yelled, laughing.

"Too bad!" Madison teased him. She glanced back. Scott actually seemed to be having fun now.

So was she. Madison charged her horse even harder. She smiled as the wind rushed though her hair. Maybe she was wrong about everything. Maybe Scott really *did* like her!

• • •

Alex wandered into the beautiful outdoor aquarium. She spotted Jordan tossing some food into a big fish tank. But he wasn't alone.

From a short distance Alex could see Jordan talking to the grumpy guy from the Sea-Doo shop. The two seemed to be in an intense conversation.

*What is Jordan doing with him?* Alex wondered.

But she didn't wait to make her move. She took a deep breath and began walking toward the aquarium. Jordan and the man stopped talking when they saw her.

"Hey, Alex," he said. "This is Champlaine." He nodded at the man. "He runs the Sea-Doo shop."

"I know," Alex said. "We've already met."

Champlaine seemed annoyed that his conversation was cut short. He glared at Alex with icy eyes, then turned back to Jordan. "So, you'll deliver that item we discussed?" he asked.

"You bet," Jordan said.

*Item?* Alex wondered. *What item?*

Champlaine glanced over his shoulder, then turned back. "Don't forget," he said, and walked away.

"What's with that guy?" Alex asked Jordan. "Why does he always look so…anxious?"

"Who knows?" Jordan shrugged.

Alex was about to ask Jordan about the mysterious *item*, when he tossed another handful of food into the tank. Three stingrays quickly ate the grub.

"They're hungry," Jordan said. "They eat four, five times a day."

"They dig in the sand for crabs, right?" Alex added.

"Yeah, they do." Jordan looked surprised. "You know about fish?"

"I love sushi," Alex joked.

Jordan laughed. Then he passed Alex a handful of food. "The fish will eat right out of your hand. Try it!"

Alex lowered her hand into the water. A stingray swam up to her and nibbled at the food. Alex petted it with her other hand. "It feels just like velvet!"

Then she pulled her hand out of the water and stared at it. It was covered with little red pucker marks. "Hey, look! The stingray gave me a hickey!"

Jordan started to laugh just as a tall bald man walked up to them. Alex thought he looked like a manager or something.

"Jordan, you're wanted at the Mayan pool," he informed them.

Jordan tossed more food into the tank. "Why don't you get Roger to do it, Stan? I'm a little busy helping this guest."

*Good thinking,* Alex thought. *We're having too much fun to be interrupted.*

"Well, I need you to help another guest now," Stan said a little impatiently. "She asked for you."

"Who is it?" Jordan asked, looking toward the Mayan pool.

Alex looked too. Lounging on a chair in front of a fake pyramid was Brianna Wallace. She was dressed in a bikini and dark sunglasses.

*Oh, great,* Alex thought as Brianna waved. *What's she going to do now?*

"Ms. Wallace's father is a very important guest," Stan told Jordan. "Let's not keep her waiting."

Stan walked briskly away. Jordan sighed. Alex could tell he was disappointed.

"I guess I'll see you later," he said to Alex.

"Hopefully sooner," Alex said.

As Jordan headed toward the pool, Alex locked eyes with Brianna.

Brianna lowered her sunglasses and winked.

Alex glared at her. She knew she would find exotic fish in the Bahamas. But she never thought she'd come face-to-face with—a shark!

# CHAPTER FIVE

Brianna lay on a beach chair by the pool, tanning her back. Jordan sighed as he spritzed her with mineral water.

*What am I?* Jordan wondered. *Some kind of personal slave?* Still, he knew he had to be polite to Brianna—or he could lose his job. "Brianna, I really should get back to work," he said.

Brianna turned around and peered at him over her sunglasses. "Is it important?"

"It's my job," he said.

"Look, as long as you're with me, you won't get into trouble. And wouldn't you rather lounge around by the pool than work at your silly old job?"

Jordan grimaced. He happened to like his job!

Stan hustled over to them. "Jordan," he said sternly. Then he stopped and added in a sweeter voice, "Sorry to disturb you, Ms. Wallace." He pulled Jordan aside. "We have an emergency and I need you right away. We have a P.I. at the shark tank."

"A P.I.?" Jordan asked.

"Puking incident," Stan explained. "A kid blew chunks in the lagoon. I need you to clean it up ASAP. I'll tell Ms. Wallace that you'll be back."

"Tell her whatever you want," Jordan said. "I'm out of here."

As he hurried off, he heard Stan say to Brianna, "Sorry to pull Jordan away."

"And what would your name and title be?" Brianna growled.

Jordan shook his head. He grabbed some rubber gloves and a pool net and headed for the shark lagoon. He scooped the net through the water, searching for signs of the P.I.

"Trolling for barf?" Alex asked him.

Jordan looked up, happy to see her. "How did you know?"

"I made the call," Alex explained.

"Then there isn't any—"

Alex shook her head no. Jordan was relieved to hear there was no mess to clean up. And he was glad to see that Alex was as clever as she was pretty.

"Isn't it about break time?" Alex asked.

Jordan nodded and grinned.

Brianna started toward the lagoon just as they were walking away. Alex lifted her sunglasses and winked at her.

• • •

After dinner that night, Griffen strolled with Madison through the grounds of Atlantis. The lights of the resort sparkled in the inky island night.

They wandered into an exhibit called The Dig. The exhibit was made to look like a real archaeological dig. The walls resembled the ruins of ancient temples. Display cases held tools and replicas of ancient statues. There was even a small-scale model of the lost city—before it got lost.

"Did you know that a lot of scholars think Atlantis was originally right here in the Caribbean?" Griffen said. He felt so comfortable with Madison. It was easy to talk to her. That was one of the things he liked about her. "Others think it was in the Mediterranean," he added.

"That's really interesting." Madison paused. "Would you mind if we talked about something a little more...personal?"

Griffen's good mood suddenly deflated. He felt sure of himself when he talked about facts. But personal things made him a little nervous. Still, he said, "Uh, no. I don't mind."

"Great." Madison led him to a bench overlooking the sea and sat down. "What I'm going to say might seem a little forward. I mean, we've known each other a long time—so I feel okay expressing this to you."

*What is she going to say?* Griffen noticed his heart was beating faster. "Express away," he said.

Madison ducked her head shyly. "Here goes," she said. "There's this guy...I think this guy likes me but he's afraid to tell me."

*Oh, boy,* Griffen thought. *She knows I like her.* "Um, maybe this guy needs you to make the first move," he said.

"That's why I'm talking to *you*," Madison replied.

Griffin's heart was pounding so hard now, he thought it might explode. He couldn't stop his mouth from breaking into a wide grin. *I don't believe it,* he thought. *She likes me too!*

"I think you know who I'm talking about," Madison went on. "It's Scott."

Griffen's stomach fell. "Scott," he said. "Of course it is. Who else could it be?"

"I don't know what to do," Madison told him. "He's always so tongue-tied. I think he needs some encouraging."

Griffen studied her face. He could see that she was confused, and he felt bad for her. "I guess you want me to talk to him," he said. *Please say no,* he thought.

She leaned over and kissed him on the cheek. "Thanks."

*Whatever it takes to help out Scott,* Griffen thought bitterly. But he knew he'd do it. Deep down, more than anything, he just wanted Madison to be happy.

"Mom and Dad wouldn't be caught dead here," Madison shouted to Alex over the noise of the band. The resort was holding a dance by one of the pools that night.

The surrounding palm trees were decorated with twinkling lights and colorful lanterns. Set up behind the diving board was a sweeping dance floor and a stage where the band played. The place was packed with kids, dancing, laughing, and having a good time.

Madison, Alex, Jordan, and Griffen were sipping fruit smoothies. Alex clinked glasses with her sister.

"This place is awesome!" Alex shouted. They stepped out on the dance floor. Brianna stepped between Alex and Jordan.

"Hey, Jordan," she said. "Want to dance?"

"Yup…" Jordan replied.

*How could he do that to Alex?* Madison thought. She felt sick when she saw Brianna smile meanly at Alex.

"…with Alex," Jordan finished.

Brianna's smile faded.

Madison grinned as Alex and Jordan disappeared into the crowd. She nodded at Griffen, and they started dancing too.

Then Madison glanced up and saw a horrific sight—Harrison, Judy, Jill, Chad, and Keegan were walking into the dance!

Alex had felt bad for ditching her parents after the water slide that morning. So she'd asked them if they wanted to hang out at the dance. But she never thought they'd show up!

"Oh, no! Our parents are here with Keegan," Madison said to Griffen.

"It's okay," Griffen assured her. "Don't panic. They're like the sun. Don't look directly at them and we'll be fine."

Madison nodded. "Right."

"Okay, we're ignoring…" Griffin said.

"And we're ignoring some more." Madison purposely turned her body away from them. "We're taking a sip of our drink, not acknowledging their presence…."

The song ended and everyone stopped dancing. Madison glanced around. "It worked! I think they left," she said.

Griffen breathed a sigh of relief.

"Now let's go see what's up with Alex," Madison suggested.

Madison and Griffen pushed their way through the packed dance floor, searching for Alex. They finally found her, standing alone in the middle of the dance floor, looking lost.

"Has anyone seen Jordan?" Alex asked, scanning the crowd. "I was just dancing with him. At least, I think I was dancing with him."

The lights dimmed and the stage went dark. Then a spotlight hit Jordan, standing center stage, holding a guitar.

Madison nudged Alex. "I think I found him."

Jordan spoke into the microphone. "I'd like to dedicate this very special song to a very special girl. Alex Stewart, this one's for you."

The spotlight searched the crowd until it found Alex. She was beaming, but Madison could tell her sister was stunned. Then the spotlight returned to the stage, and Jordan began to sing a romantic song.

Griffen and Madison exchanged warm smiles. Then Griffen looked uncomfortable and glanced away.

Madison felt uncomfortable too. But she didn't know why.

When the song was over, the crowd applauded wildly. Alex rushed up to the stage and threw her arms around Jordan.

Madison felt happy for Alex. Then she heard someone behind her mutter, "Well, well, well. Isn't love grand?"

Turning, Madison spotted Brianna. She was twisting the straw in her smoothie between her fingers as she glared at the stage.

A shiver ran up Madison's spine. One look at Brianna's face told her that she meant business. Nasty business.

She thought of warning Alex but reconsidered. She didn't want to do anything that would ruin this moment for Alex. And she hoped that Brianna wouldn't either!

# CHAPTER SIX

The next morning was beautiful and sunny. Griffen walked through the grounds of Atlantis until he came to the pool. A tan, muscular guy was swimming laps alone in the water. It was Scott. Just the person Griffen was looking for.

*Oh, well,* he said to himself. *A promise is a promise....* He squatted at the edge of the pool.

Scott swam up, touched the cement edge, and popped up for air.

"What's up?" Griffen asked as Scott pulled himself out of the water.

"Do I know you, dude?" Scott asked.

"Sort of," Griffen replied. "I'm a friend of Madison's."

Scott stopped. He stared at Griffen. "You going with her?"

*I wish,* Griffen thought. "We're only friends."

"Good," Scott said. "'Cause I'm really into her. But I have trouble talking to her, you know? I think she thinks I'm an idiot."

Griffen paused, not sure how to respond. Personally, he thought Scott was a little lacking in the brain-power department. But he seemed like a nice enough guy. "No, I doubt it," Griffen finally said. "She doesn't think you're an idiot."

"It's like when I'm with her, I freeze," Scott explained. "Not the teeth-chattering type of freeze, you know, the, uh—"

Griffen cut him off. "I think I know what you mean. Just go with me on this, okay?"

Scott nodded.

"I know exactly what to say to a girl," Griffen said. "I have all the words in my head. But there's something about her—the girl, I mean—and I just can't say it."

"Exactly!" Scott agreed. "Except it's the opposite for me. I don't have any problem saying whatever I want to a girl. The problem is I don't have much to say. And I'm meeting Madison in a couple of hours. I mean, how am I supposed to come up with something to talk about *and* finish my workout at the same time?

*I can't believe I'm about to do this*, Griffen thought. "Scott, I think might be able to help you...."

• • •

"Let me tell you a little something about our target," Griffen said a half hour later. He was sitting beside Scott in the weight room. Scott was pumping iron at the free weight bench. Griffen was talking about his favorite subject—Madison.

"She likes astronomy," Griffen said. "And when she was growing up, she loved Judy Blume books. Have you read any Judy Blume books?"

Scott grunted as he lifted the weights.

"Have you ready *any* books?" Griffen asked.

Scott lowered the weights to the floor. "Does *Sports Illustrated* count?"

"That would be a magazine," Griffen said. "Try to remember these titles. *Blubber.*"

"*Blubber,*" Scott repeated.

"*Forever.*"

"*Forever,*" Scott echoed, though he didn't seem to know what he was saying.

"She loves that book," Griffen added.

"If she loves it, I love it," Scott declared.

"Good," Griffen said. "I've given you a number of topics to discuss with her—guaranteed to break the ice. Are you ready?"

Scott tapped his forehead with his finger. "I've got it all here in a nutshell," he said.

"Uh—yeah," Griffen said. *He'll never get this stuff*

*right,* he thought. But deep down, Griffen was afraid Scott *would* get it right. Too right.

"I had a great time horseback riding the other day," Madison said to Scott. They were walking hand in hand down the beach. "Did you?"

Scott opened his mouth to speak but said nothing. Madison didn't really know what to say either.

"It's...hot," she declared.

"Yeah," Scott said.

"Glad I wore sunscreen," Madison added.

"Yeah," Scott said.

Madison sighed. "Scott?"

"Yeah?" he replied.

"Are you okay?"

"Yeah. Why do you ask?"

Madison rolled her eyes. Talking to Scott was as easy as doing a headstand on a pyramid! *Maybe we just have nothing in common.*

"Um, Madison?" Scott asked. "When do we start talking about books?"

Madison lifted her sunglasses and stared at Scott. "What?" She was pleasantly surprised. "If you want to talk about books, great. I love books."

"Okay. Here goes." Scott cleared his throat. "Tell me, Madison. Do you like to read?"

Madison was puzzled. Didn't she just say that she loved books? *Maybe this is leading to a joke or something,* she thought. *I'll go along with it.* "Um, yes, I like to read," she said. "Do you?"

"I like Judy Blume," Scott declared.

Madison stopped dead in her tracks. "You're kidding!" she cried. "She was my favorite author when I was a kid. What have you read by her?"

"*Flubber,*" Scott said.

"*Flubber?*" Madison giggled a little.

Scott's eyes darted nervously from side to side. "Was that wrong?"

*He looks so cute when he's nervous,* Madison thought. "Only by one letter. The title is *Blubber.*"

"Right. Hey, do you read *Sports Illustrated?*"

*Sports and Judy Blume,* Madison thought. *This guy has a wide range of interests.*

But the Judy Blume stuff bothered her a little. He didn't get the title of the book right. Did he really read it? She'd never met a guy like Scott who was into that kind of stuff.

Still, she thought, he couldn't be making it up. How could he possibly know that she liked Judy Blume?

# CHAPTER SEVEN

*Jordan is so perfect,* Alex thought as she gazed through the window of the hotel dining room. She and Madison were having lunch with their parents and the Graysons.

Alex sighed and pushed around the salad on her plate. She'd had so much fun hanging out with him and feeding the stingrays. She couldn't wait to see him again. They planned to meet for a walk on the beach that night. A *romantic* walk, she hoped.

"So what do you kids have planned after lunch?" Harrison asked.

*Thinking about the boy of my dreams,* Alex thought. But she wasn't about to tell Dad that. "We're going to hit the beach," Alex told him. "Then, after a while, we're going to check out the other beach. How about you?"

"Keegan and I are going to make a sand castle," Harrison said. "Right, Keegan?"

Keegan held up a detailed drawing on a napkin. "Blueprints are done. I'm ready, Mr. Stewart."

"I'm going into town," Judy said. "I think it will be fun. Want to go, girls?"

"To town?" Alex echoed.

"What's in town?" Madison asked.

Judy flashed her credit card. "Shopping."

Alex felt a little shiver of pleasure. "Shopping. What a beautiful word."

"Mom, you're inspired," Madison added.

"Hey—that's not fair," Harrison said to his wife.

"You can come shopping with us if you want," Judy told him. "We might even let you carry the bags."

"On second thought, I'll stay here," Harrison said. "How are you planning to get into town?"

Alex and Madison looked at each other. They had the same thought at once. "Mopeds!"

After lunch, the girls and their mother putted into town on rented mopeds. *I can't wait to get my driver's license,* Alex thought as she rode. Driving herself around was the ultimate independence!

They parked their mopeds in the center of town and took off their helmets.

Judy shook out her short blond hair. "Okay. What do we want to see first?"

"Everything!" Madison and Alex said together.

In the clothing bazaar they tried on colorful

Caribbean dresses and straw hats. They paused to watch a man carve candles into beautiful shapes. They saw women weaving fancy baskets. Then they stopped at a stall selling Caribbean artifacts. Madison picked up a small ancient-looking wooden statue.

"Wow, is this real?" she asked.

"No," Judy replied. "It's illegal to sell the real stuff. They're considered national treasures. All native artifacts sold here are replicas. Do you want to buy it?"

"Pass," Madison said, putting the statue down.

At last they stopped at an outdoor café to get something to drink. A waiter delivered three raspberry smoothies to their table.

"So, how is the vacation going?" Judy asked.

"I'm having an awful time with Scott," Madison reported. "I *think* we have a connection, but he kind of gets tongue-tied a lot."

"I've had the best time with Jordan," Alex said. "I got a hickey from a stingray!"

"That *does* sound like fun," Judy said. She pulled a map from her straw bag and began studying it.

Alex gazed across the plaza. Too bad things weren't working out for Madison and Scott as well as they were with her and Jordan.

Then she saw something that surprised her.

Jordan was crossing the plaza with a package under his arm.

Alex nudged Madison. Madison glanced across the plaza. She started to say something, but Alex stopped her. Something didn't feel right about this.

Jordan stopped at a table full of shady-looking men. He handed the package to a man with white hair at the table. Alex recognized him—it was Champlaine.

Champlaine looked over his shoulders as he took the package. Then he practically ignored Jordan as he shook hands with the other men.

Alex turned to Madison. "What do you think is inside that package?" she whispered.

"I don't know," Madison whispered back. "Why don't you ask him when you see him?"

"Why don't I ask him now?" Alex said. She gazed across the plaza again. But Champlaine's seat was empty now. And Jordan was gone.

"Everything all right?" Judy asked, looking up from her map.

"Yeah, Mom," Alex said. "Everything is fine."

But after seeing Jordan with creepy Champlaine again, she wasn't so sure.

# CHAPTER EIGHT

"So how'd it go with Madison?" Griffen asked. He was back in the weight room with Scott while Madison and Alex were shopping.

Scott didn't answer. He was grunting and pumping two-hundred-pound weights.

*Look at him,* Griffen thought. *Does he think that Madison likes guys with pumped up pecs?* Then he had a scary thought. What if she did?

He reached for a twenty-pounder. "Oof!" Griffen grunted. It was heavier than he thought.

Scott lowered his weights and sat up. He looked troubled. "I think it went great, but I found out something about myself I didn't know."

"What's that?" Griffen asked.

"My memory stinks. The situation is desperate."

Griffen leaned forward. "Talk to me."

That night after dinner, Griffen hid behind a column near the aquarium, waiting for Scott and Madison to show up.

"I can't believe I'm doing this," he muttered. He glanced down at the stack of cue cards at his feet.

When he glanced back up, he saw Madison and Scott coming. Madison was trying to look at the fish in the huge tank. But Scott kept pulling her along as if he had to get somewhere.

"Hey, what's the rush?" Madison asked. "It was your idea to come here."

"I just want to—to say something," Scott said.

He sat her down on a bench near the column where Griffen was hiding. He positioned Madison so that her back was to Griffen.

Griffen peeked out from behind the column and nodded to Scott. *Good,* he thought. *Scott has a clear view of me.* He picked up the stack of cue cards and pointed to the first one. Scott squinted to read it.

*Don't make it too obvious,* Griffen thought. Sure enough, Madison tried to turn around to see what Scott was looking at. Griffen ducked back behind the column.

Scott turned her to face him again. He took her hand, still struggling to read Griffen's cue card.

"'The soul selects her own society,'" Scott read. "'Then shuts the door; On her divine majority, Obtrude no more.'"

Madison smiled. "That's Emily Dickinson,

51

right?" she said. "I really love her work."

"Me too," Scott said.

*Yeah, right,* Griffen thought as he changed cue cards.

Scott squinted again. "Do you like astronomy?" he asked Madison.

"I love astronomy," Madison said.

"Me too," Scott agreed. "What's your sign?"

"That's astrology," Madison corrected him.

"Oh." Desperate, Scott struggled to see the cue cards. But a group of tourists stepped in front of the column. They stared into the fish tank, oohing and ahhing—and blocking Scott's view of Griffen.

Griffen jumped around, trying to show the cue cards to Scott. He tried to weave around the tourists, but their group was too big. And Griffen didn't want to risk getting caught by Madison.

*Come on, come on,* Griffen thought. *Get out of the way!*

But they didn't budge. Griffen peered through the crowd. He could tell that Scott was panicking.

"Uhhh...I have to go to the bathroom," Scott blurted out. He leaped to his feet and bolted away, leaving Madison alone.

*Great,* Griffen thought. *Way to go, Scott.*

• • •

"How did you get away from your folks?" Jordan asked Alex as they strolled down the moonlit beach.

"I didn't," Alex said. "They think I'm in my room."

Alex felt Jordan take her hand. "Has anybody ever told you you're incredible?" he asked her.

Alex blushed. They gazed at the moon. It was so romantic, but Alex couldn't stop thinking about that package. What was in it? *I should just ask him about it,* Alex decided. She turned to Jordan.

Jordan stared deep into Alex's eyes. "Has anybody ever told you that I'm going to kiss you?"

*Kiss me?* Alex's knees started shaking. Jordan leaned forward and she shut her eyes. *Jordan is going to kiss me! He's going to kiss me!*

*Don't you dare kiss her,* Brianna thought as she watched from behind a palm tree. She forced herself to look as Jordan's and Alex's lips came together in a soft, sweet romantic kiss.

Brianna wanted to scream. *Doesn't he realize that Alex is a loser?* she thought. *A total loser?*

Brianna watched bitterly as Jordan and Alex gently pulled apart. They joined hands and continued down the beach.

*Well,* Brianna thought. *I guess it's up to me to show him.*

# CHAPTER NINE

"What's the matter?" Alex asked Madison later that night. She'd come into the room after her date with Jordan and found Madison lying on her bed, looking bummed out.

"I don't know what to do about Scott." Madison replied. "I like him, but every time we get together he's a total boulder." She sighed. "Maybe it's my problem. Maybe I'm the one who doesn't know what to say to guys."

Alex frowned. She hated seeing Madison in the dumps. "Hey!" Alex said. She grabbed Madison's arm and pulled her off the bed. "Why don't you come with Jordan and me for a little late-night water slide action."

Madison grabbed a towel off the chair. "I think that's just what I need."

In the hallway, Madison stopped by Griffen's door. She knocked lightly.

Griffen opened the door. "What's up?" he asked.

"Water slide," Madison said. "Are you in?"

Griffen smiled. "You bet!"

The three of them met Jordan at the Leap of Faith water slide. After whooshing down, they splashed and laughed in the pool. Then Alex ducked down under the surface. When she came back up for air, she found herself bathed in the beam of a flashlight.

"What's going on?" she asked, blinking.

A security guard was holding the flashlight. "Tell Ms. Wallace we found the noise problem," he said into a walkie-talkie.

"Ms. Wallace?" Madison repeated. "As in—"

Alex spotted a dark-haired girl standing halfway behind the lifeguard station. In her hand was a cell phone. And on her face was a triumphant grin.

"Brianna," Alex muttered.

"Out of the pool, now." the security guard said.

He led them to the security office, locked the door, and left. The four of them sat in the office for fifteen minutes, waiting to see what would happen.

At last the security guard returned. "Jordan Landers—you can go," he said.

"I can?" Jordan asked.

"Ms. Wallace doesn't want you to get into trouble," the guard explained.

"What about my friends?" Jordan asked.

"She didn't say anything about them," the guard

replied. "They'll have to stay here."

Jordan folded his arms across his chest and sat down. "Then I'm staying too."

The guard pushed Jordan toward the door. "Out. I'm serious." Jordan glanced back at Alex, but the guard closed the door in his face.

Alex sat there, fuming. It was just like Brianna to do something so mean.

The phone rang. The security guard answered it. He nodded and hung up.

"Okay, kids," he said. "You can go."

"Great!" Alex said.

The security guard opened the door. On the other side were Harrison, Judy, Chad, and Jill—all scowling.

Alex gulped. "I take that back."

"But, Dad—we can explain," Alex pleaded. She and Madison were in bed. Her parents stood by the door of their room. Alex couldn't stand the "we're so disappointed in you" look on their faces.

"No, you can't," Harrison said. "Good night."

He and Judy left the room, closing the door behind them.

"Wow," Madison said. "They're really upset."

"Yeah," Alex said. "But I bet they'll be over it by the morning."

When Alex woke up the next morning, the sun was shining brightly into their room. She glanced at the clock. It was 10:45!

Alex looked over at Madison, who was rubbing the sleep from her eyes. "That's weird," she said. "We didn't get the usual eight-thirty A.M. wake-up call from Mom and Dad."

Someone knocked on the door.

"That must be them," Madison said. "A personal wake-up call."

She got up and opened the door. It was Griffen.

"Hey," he said. He grabbed a note that was taped to their door and ripped it off. "I guess you haven't seen this yet." He handed the note to Madison. "I got the same one."

Madison read the note. "'Went to have fun. Love, Mom and Dad.'" She looked at Alex, who shrugged.

"I don't believe it," Madison said. "Mom and Dad ditched us!"

Alex ran to the window and stared out at the ocean. "Could that be them out there?" she asked, pointing to three specks in a speedboat and two specks wakeboarding on the ocean. "Isn't that Mom's red bikini?"

"Let's go down and see," Madison said. They dressed quickly and hurried down to the beach.

Harrison, Judy, Jill, Chad, and Keegan were riding to shore in a motorboat, whooping and hollering and having a great time.

"Excuse me, but are parents supposed to have that much fun?" Alex grumbled.

The parents and Keegan headed to shore and dropped their wakeboards on the sand.

"Hey, guys," Chad waved to them. "How ya doin'?"

"We didn't hear from you this morning," Madison said.

"Oh, yeah, sorry," Harrison said. "We just wanted to get an early start."

"Honey, we've got snorkeling in ten minutes," Judy reminded him.

"Right." The parents and Keegan began to head for the snorkel center.

"You guys are okay with getting lunch on your own, right?" Judy asked.

"Uh, sure," Alex said.

"Great. We'll catch you later."

Alex stared in disbelief as they walked away, laughing and talking. She waited for them to look back and wave, but they didn't.

"Well, this is what we wanted, right?" Madison said. "Independence. They're letting us have it at last."

# CHAPTER TEN

Alex, Griffen, and Madison decided to meet Jordan outside the Sea-Doo shack. They were all going to ride out to Dolphin Island to hang with the dolphins.

"Where's Jordan?" Alex asked.

"He's renting the Sea-Doos for us," Madison said. "It looks like he's trying to talk down the price."

Alex watched Jordan through the window. He was talking to Champlaine and waving his arms around. Champlaine was shaking his head no.

*What's going on with them?* Alex wondered if it was about that package. Was he making a deal to deliver another one?

Finally, Jordan left the shack and hurried over to them. "Forty bucks for all of us," he announced.

"Awesome!" Madison cried.

"I told you." Jordan smiled. "I got connections."

*Connections?* Alex wondered. That did it. She had to ask him what the deal was with Champlaine. "I noticed," she said. "That's why I've got to ask you this. What were you doing in town yesterday?"

"You were there?" Jordan asked.

"We were shopping and we saw you," Madison said. She nodded at Champlaine. "Talking to him."

"Champlaine? I was just doing him a favor and delivering a package. And now he's helping us out."

"But what was in the package?" Alex asked.

Jordan shrugged. "Probably something boring," he said. "Like guava jelly."

"I love guava jelly!" Griffen piped in.

*That makes sense, I guess...* Alex thought. She trusted Jordan, but somehow she didn't believe the package held jelly. Maybe it was because she didn't trust Champlaine. But just because she didn't like the looks of the guy didn't mean she could accuse him of something.

"All right," Alex said, nodding at the Sea-Doos. "Let's bounce."

Later that day, Griffen visited the shark tank by himself. It was great hanging out with Madison, Alex, and Jordan, and swimming with the dolphins. Too bad they weren't into sharks too.

"Yo, Grif!" a voice called.

Griffen spun around and saw a desperate-looking Scott. He rushed over to Griffen, holding a paper shopping bag in one hand.

"Madison wants to meet me at the Café in an hour," Scott said with a pleading tone in his voice.

Griffen got the message. "Oh, no," he said. "The last date we went on totally tanked!"

"But this plan is foolproof," Scott said. He opened his shopping bag to show Griffen a mini-microphone and earphone with a battery pack and a walkie-talkie.

Griffen stared at the walkie-talkie. Scott had to be desperate if he was going to all this trouble. Maybe he really did care about Madison.

"All right," Griffen agreed. "But you've got to do exactly as I tell you."

Griffen took a table at the Café, a causal outdoor restaurant at the resort. He hid behind his menu while Scott guided Madison to a table on the other side of the restaurant.

Scott pulled out a chair for Madison. Griffen peeked around his menu and saw that Madison was about to sit down facing him.

"Don't let her sit there," Griffen said into the walkie-talkie. Did he have to tell Scott everything? "She'll see me!"

Scott quickly pulled the chair away and sat

down in it himself. Madison shot him a strange look. "What's the matter?" she asked.

Griffen spoke into the walkie-talkie. "Tell her the sun sets in the west and I wanted you to have the better view."

"The sun sets in the west and I wanted you to have the better view," Scott repeated.

"You're so sweet." Madison sat down next to him. She could probably see Griffen if she turned her head, but at least she wasn't facing him anymore.

"Yes, I am," Scott said.

"Tell her you read a really great book the other day," Griffen said into the walkie-talkie.

"I read a really great book the other day," Scott said.

"What book was that?" Madison asked.

A waitress approached Griffen and asked for his order. Griffen glanced at the menu and said to the waitress, "The grilled chicken."

"The grilled chicken," Scott obediently repeated.

*Oops!* Griffen thought. He'd accidentally spoken into the walkie-talkie when he ordered. And that chowderhead was repeating everything he said without thinking.

"I've never heard of that book," Madison said.

It was the last day of school before winter break. I could not stop day-dreaming about our class trip to Hawaii. It was going to be our first vacation without our parents!

I caught Alex daydreaming too.
Doesn't she have a goofy look on her face?

Then Mom and Dad whisked us off to the Bahamas. We weren't happy about missing Hawaii, but we were going to make the best of it.

Vacation with
our parents and
the Grayson
family wasn't so
bad after all.

We got to ride
Sea-Doos . . .

And we even swam with the dolphins!

We also hung out a lot with Griffen Grayson. He's kind of cute, isn't he? I had no idea he had a crush on me!

This is Scott, and I had a crush on him. But I soon found out we had nothing in common.

Alex met a cute boy named Jordan. Here he is, showing her how to S.C.U.B.A. dive. Alex really likes him.

I found someone I really like too—Griffen! Can you believe Alex snapped this picture just as he was about to kiss me?

This was definitely one family vacation to remember. Let's hope next year's is just as cool!

Griffen had to work fast to cover up Scott's dumb mistake.

"It's a mystery," he said to Scott. "A series, actually. The Grilled Chicken, the Fried Sparrow, the Cooked Goose..."

Scott repeated what Griffen said. Madison looked at him strangely.

"You're kidding me, right?" she said. "A mystery series about different ways to cook birds? Scott are you feeling okay?"

"Tell her you didn't sleep much, as the mere thought of spending the day with her made you twitch in anticipation," Griffen instructed.

"I didn't sleep 'cause the mere thought of hangin' with you made me itch in anticipation," Scott echoed.

"Not *itch*, you idiot!" Griffen scolded.

"Not itch, you idiot!" Scott shouted at Madison.

"What?" Madison looked insulted. "Who are you talking to?"

"*Twitch! Twitch!*" Griffen corrected Scott.

"Twitch! Twitch!" Scott repeated.

"Sometimes you say the weirdest things," Madison said, her brow wrinkled with confusion.

The waitress brought Griffen his plate of chicken. "Thanks," Griffen said to her—and into the walkie-talkie.

"Thanks," Scott said.

Madison frowned. She gave Scott her penetrating stare. Griffen recognized it. *Uh-oh,* he thought. *She's on to us....*

"Scott, I don't know what your problem is," she said. "But I think you should...go to the bathroom!"

Madison jumped up from her chair. As she headed out of the restaurant, she passed Griffen's table. He tried to hide the walkie-talkie in his roll basket. Too late.

Madison was staring at him—and his walkie-talkie!

"Um." Griffen forced a smile as he held up the walkie-talkie. "I was just telling my folks to order the grilled chicken—I mean, the coconut island shrimp. Whatever."

Madison didn't say a word. She walked out of the restaurant.

*Great,* Griffen thought. *Even if I did have the guts to ask her out, she'd never say yes now. How could I be such a jerk?*

# CHAPTER ELEVEN

Madison found Griffen throwing stones into the bay. It was only an hour after the restaurant disaster, and the sun was beginning to set.

"Scott told me everything," she said.

"I don't know what you're talking about," Griffen tried to bluff.

"Look, I'm straight up with you," Madison said. "You be straight up with me."

Griffen dropped the stone in his hand and nodded. "All right—you got me."

"This is really my fault," Madison said, smiling. "I asked you to encourage Scott. I just didn't expect you to *be* him."

"I guess I got carried away," Griffen admitted. "All I wanted to do was make you happy."

Madison smiled. "You did."

"I...did?"

Madison nodded. Then she tilted her head. "How come you know so much about me, Griffen?"

"Everyone's got a hobby, right?" He blushed.

"I guess that you're mine."

Madison smiled. That was the sweetest thing anyone had ever said to her. She pulled him close and gave him a big kiss. "Judy Blume?" she said. "That goes back a few years."

"I've had a crush on you for a long time." Griffen took her hand and they began to walk along the shore. "Did you know Antares is in the southern sky all night this summer?" He pointed skyward.

"Really? That's fantastic," Madison said.

"It's the second largest red giant in our galaxy."

"*Second* largest?" Madison said. "No, I'm pretty sure it's the largest."

"I think you're right...."

Madison sighed happily. At last someone she could talk to! At last someone who could *talk*!

Madison and Alex got dressed for the evening. A room service cart filled with empty plates and glasses sat near the door of their room.

"Running up Dad's room service tab alone in our room isn't the same as eating in the restaurant with Mom and Dad," Madison complained. "I miss them telling us what to do."

"We deserve this," Alex said. "We totally brushed them off this trip. Now look at us. We're going out tonight and they don't even care."

Someone knocked at the door. Madison opened it, and there stood Griffen. Madison hugged him.

Alex grinned. She couldn't remember the last time Madison looked so happy. And with Griffen's black T-shirt and gray cargo shorts, she couldn't remember when he looked so cute!

Alex grabbed her bag. "Come on, you guys," she said. "Jordan wants us to meet him at the dock. He said he has a huge surprise for me."

"Hmmm. A surprise," Madison said as she slipped on her sneakers. "Looks like you won the war against Brianna." She grabbed her backpack and they were out the door.

They all headed for the dock, where a sleek white speedboat waited for them. Jordan stood at the wheel.

"Jordan, you are amazing!" Alex cried. "Let's go. I can't wait to see what the island looks like from offshore at night."

Griffen helped the girls aboard the boat.

"We've got to make one little stop on the way back," Jordan told them. "Champlaine wants me to pick something up for some high roller."

*Champlaine again!* Alex thought.

Jordan throttled the engine and they sped off.

They cruised around the bay under the stars. Alex watched the moonlight ripple on the water.

After a while, a huge, spectacular yacht loomed ahead of them, anchored half a mile from the shore. Jordan slowed the speedboat down.

"Is that our little stop?" Alex asked.

"Yup," Jordan replied. "You don't mind, do you?"

"No problem," Alex said. She'd never seen a yacht like that before. It was like a mansion on the water.

Jordan moored the speedboat to the yacht and stepped on the gangplank. "Welcome aboard the *Starling*," he said. "This won't take long."

All four of them climbed aboard and looked around. A red-and-black flag flapped in the breeze from atop a tall mast. Otherwise, everything was quiet.

"Make yourselves at home," Jordan said. "But don't touch anything. I'll be right back." He disappeared into a cabin below deck.

"Anybody notice what's missing from this boat?" Madison asked.

"A party?" Griffen suggested.

"No," Madison said. "People."

"You're right," Alex agreed. "It's deserted." She looked at Madison and Griffen. Were they thinking what she was thinking?

"Let's explore!" Madison said excitedly.

They climbed the stairs below deck and found a luxurious dining room set for dinner for twelve. The plates were covered with caviar and other fancy hors d'oeuvres.

"Wow," Griffen gasped.

Alex swiped a taste of caviar. "Well, we found the party."

Madison backed up and bumped into a built-in stereo system. Her back pushed a button. Classical music—Mozart—blared from the speakers. She quickly whirled around and switched the music off.

"I don't think I've ever heard Mozart that loud before," she said.

"Wonder who owns this tub?" Griffen said.

"I thought I heard you guys in here." Jordan entered the room, carrying two fishing rods and a fancy tackle box. "Some rich guy owns this thing," he said.

"I thought you needed to pick something up, not go fishing," Alex said to Jordan.

"This is it." Jordan grinned. "The owner is probably stuck in the casino. He needed his fishing rig first thing in the morning. Maybe he's going out on another ship tomorrow."

They loaded the fishing gear onto the speedboat

and zoomed back to the dock. As they got out of the boat, Jordan said, "Wait here. I just need to bring this gear over to—"

Suddenly a bright light blinded them. A man's voice boomed through a megaphone. "You will all stand perfectly still."

Alex shielded her eyes from the light and looked toward the beach. A dozen police officers stood on the shore in front of several police cars.

Alex gasped. What was going on?

Two police officers grabbed Jordan and snatched the tackle box away from him.

"Hey!" Jordan cried. "That doesn't belong to you!"

"Quite correct," one policeman said. He opened the tackle box. Alex stepped closer to look inside.

It wasn't filled with fishing gear at all. It was filled with delicately carved statuettes.

"This belongs to the people of the Bahamas," the policeman declared. "And you are under arrest for smuggling priceless antiquities." He glared at Griffen, Madison, and Alex. "All of you."

# CHAPTER TWELVE

"You know," Jordan said, looking around. "This is really a nice jail. They've got TV, magazines..."

"Are you serious?" Madison groaned.

Alex, Jordan, Madison, and Griffen all shared a cell inside the police station.

"We're sitting here in jail, Jordan," Griffen grumbled. "And it's all your fault."

"I didn't know," Jordan protested. "I swear."

"It was a setup," Madison grumbled.

"Hey, lay off," Alex said. "If he says he didn't know, he didn't know."

Madison stared at Alex. "Alex, do you realize where we are?" she cried. "This isn't detention. This is jail! In a foreign country! And you're saying we should *trust* Jordan?"

Alex gazed at Jordan. "Yes."

Madison groaned under her breath. Just a few hours ago she was enjoying her first moonlight cruise with Griffen.

Now they were spending their first date in jail.

•  •  •

The next morning, the Stewart and Grayson parents arrived to pick up their kids. Alex cringed at the sight of them. They were clearly upset.

Alex, Madison, and Griffen were released from jail into their parents' custody. An investigator walked with the adults as they left the jail.

"Thanks for understanding, Officer," Harrison said.

"We are satisfied the kids had no prior knowledge of the crime," the investigator said. He turned to Griffen and the girls and added, "But you should learn to choose your companions more wisely."

This made Alex angry. "We do," she snapped. "And that's why we know Jordan isn't guilty."

"At least we hope not," Madison whispered.

"Good day," the investigator said. He left them at the door of the station. The two families stepped out into the bright sunshine.

"We need to have a family meeting," Harrison announced.

"You better believe it," Chad said.

"But don't you see—they're blaming Jordan and it wasn't his fault!" Alex was frustrated that no one would listen to her. "Why aren't they letting *him* out of jail like the rest of us?"

"Honey, he was caught red-handed," Judy objected.

"He didn't know what was in the tackle box," Alex insisted. "We told the police the tackle box was on a big yacht in the bay, but they didn't want to listen. Why aren't they looking on the yacht instead of blaming everything on Jordan?"

Alex watched carefully as her mother looked at her father. Would they believe her?

"Okay," Harrison said at last. "Where is this yacht?"

They all hurried to the dock. Alex shaded her eyes, straining to spot the gigantic white yacht in the bay. But it was gone.

Madison looked just as confused. "It was right here last night," she said slowly.

*Oh, no,* Alex thought. Her parents were shaking their heads as if she, Madison, and Griffen had made the whole thing up!

Then Alex had an idea.

"Champlaine," she gasped. "The white-haired guy."

"Right!" Madison agreed.

"Dad, we know who'll clear this whole thing up," Alex said. "Jordan did a favor for him last night. He owns the Sea-Doo shack on the beach."

She gazed up at her father, pleading with her eyes for his help. She knew he couldn't resist.

"All right." Harrison sighed.

They rushed across the beach toward the Sea-Doo shack. But that was gone too!

"It was right here!" Alex exclaimed. She stared in disbelief. Now there was nothing but sand.

Harrison put his arm around her shoulder. "Let's go to the Café and have a private family meeting," he suggested.

Alex, Madison, Harrison, and Judy sat outside at the Café, talking things over.

"Look, we trust you," Harrison said to the girls. "You're good girls. We let you run around on your own. But you know what? We just bailed you out of jail. The rest of the vacation, you're sticking with us."

Alex and Madison opened their mouths to protest. Before either one could say a word, their father added, "And there's no discussion."

Alex slumped in her seat. Their vacation was ruined. And worst of all—Jordan was in big trouble.

"I can't believe it." Griffen sat with Alex and Madison on a bench overlooking the sea. "We got turned into leash babies."

It was just minutes after the Stewart family meeting. The kids were having a meeting of their own.

"Yeah," Madison said. "How are we going to

clear Jordan if we're stuck with Mom and Dad?"

Alex was glad to hear that her sister was on her side. "So you believe Jordan didn't do it?"

"The graffiti is on the wall," Madison said. "This is a major cover-up. We've got to find that slimeball Champlaine—and that yacht."

Alex reached out her right hand. The other two covered her hand with theirs. They made a pact.

"But what about Mom and Dad?" Alex asked. "They'll be watching our every move."

"If we always know where they are, then we'll never miss an opportunity to escape," Griffen said. Then he nodded. "Let's do it."

Alex glanced up at the parents. Harrison and Judy were lying by the pool on lounge chairs, reading. Chad and Jill were dozing nearby. Alex, Madison, and Keegan were splashing each other and making a racket in the pool. Alex glanced at Griffen. He was secretly recording the sounds they made.

Griffen ran a finger across his throat—the signal to cut the noise. The kids stood quietly in the pool. But the tape recorder played, so it sounded as if they were still laughing and splashing.

Griffen handed the recorder to Keegan. "Do you want to be on the team?" he asked her.

"More than life itself," she replied.

"There can't be any slipups," he warned.

"It's not rocket science, bro," she cracked.

"All right—go," Alex said.

Keegan moved closer to the adults, tape recorder in hand. She carefully flicked a switch, and sounds of the noisy pool filled the air. Alex, Madison, and Griffen swam silently to the other side of the pool and slipped away.

They sneaked off to the front of the hotel, hopped on some mopeds, and were off!

They rode into town, looking for Champlaine. They drove from the cafés in the plaza to the busy marketplace.

Walking from stall to stall, they searched the crowd for the white-haired man. At last Madison spotted him at an art merchant's stall.

"There he is," she cried. He was doing some kind of business with the merchant. When he spotted the kids, he dropped what he was doing and ran away.

"Where did he go?" Alex asked. They scoured the packed marketplace. Then they heard a moped rev up. They ran around to the back of a rug stall.

"There he is!" Alex cried. "And he's getting away!" Champlaine sped away on a moped, heading toward the bay. Griffen, Alex, and Madison hopped onto their mopeds and chased after him.

"He's headed for the docks!" Griffen called. "Hurry!"

They reached the docks and looked around. No sign of him.

"Which way did he go?" Griffen asked.

"Quiet!" said Alex. "Do you hear his moped?"

Just then they heard the loud blare of a ship's horn. They looked up to see a huge white cruise ship pulling out of the harbor. Standing on the top deck was Champlaine, coolly waving good-bye to them.

Alex slumped on her moped. "Well, that's it."

"No, it isn't," Madison said. "We can still look for the yacht."

Griffen checked his watch. "But we just ran out of time. We've got to get back before our parents figure out we're gone."

Alex blinked back tears as they mounted their mopeds and returned to Atlantis. She just knew Jordan was innocent. If only there was a way to prove it!

# CHAPTER THIRTEEN

"Mom, Dad, isn't it time for lunch?" Alex asked.

Alex, Madison, and Griffen had sneaked back into the pool. Keegan cut the tape of their noisy playing. Their parents hadn't missed them.

Harrison looked up from his book. "Good idea."

Chad and Jill stirred in their lounge chairs. "Why don't you kids dry off and meet us at the Café in five minutes."

"That's a hard five minutes," Harrison warned.

"Okay, Dad," Alex said. She waited until the adults were gone. "The guy on that yacht must be filthy rich," she said to Griffen, Madison, and Keegan. "He can't be smuggling artifacts for the money."

"Then he must be a collector," Madison reasoned.

"So if there was one antiquity, there will be more," Griffen concluded. "And that's all we need to get Jordan out of jail."

Alex was more determined than ever. "We've got to find that boat."

• • •

Five minutes later, everyone met for lunch at the Café. Madison nodded at Alex. *Time to start the plan.*

"Ohhh…" Alex moaned as if her stomach hurt.

"What's wrong?" Madison asked.

"I think I swallowed too much water," Alex said, clutching her stomach. "I don't feel so good."

"I'll take you to the ladies' room," Madison helped her to her feet. "We'll be right back," she said to her parents. Then she turned to Griffen. "Why don't you go to the hotel pharmacy and see if they have any Pepto-Bismol?"

"Good idea." Griffen rose to his feet.

Griffen headed to the left. Madison and Alex went right. They all met in front of the hotel.

Griffen grabbed Madison and gave her a quick kiss. "Wow!" she gasped. "What was that for?"

"Just in case I end up in jail and don't get another chance," Griffen said. He took her hand. "Come on."

They hurried back to the docks, searching for the yacht. "Maybe we should check with the harbormaster," Madison suggested.

Griffen shook his head. "It'll draw too much attention to us. We're on our own here."

Way down the pier, Madison spotted something familiar—a red-and-black flag. "Hey," she said. "Didn't the *Starling* fly a red-and-black flag on her high mast?" She pointed to the flag in the distance.

"You're right," Griffen said. "Maybe that's the *Starling*!"

They hurried down the dock until they reached the yacht with the red and black flag. It looked a lot like the *Starling*—except the name painted on the side was *Saxon Explorer*.

"*Saxon Explorer*?" Griffen said. "That's not the right name."

"Let's check it out anyway," Madison suggested. "If they can move her, they can change her name."

They started carefully down the slip toward the gangway. A man appeared on the deck.

*Oh, no,* Madison thought. *Someone's on board.*

They stopped and sat on a bench, pretending to be watching the boats in the harbor.

The man hurried down the gangway and off the yacht. He was a dashing gray-haired man in his fifties. He wore crisp white pants, a dark blue polo shirt, and tan leather moccasins.

*He looks slick,* Madison thought as he stalked by. *Slick and dangerous.*

The man headed toward the yacht club and disappeared. "Perfect," Alex whispered. "Let's go."

They slipped onto the yacht and sneaked below deck. Madison scanned the place. There was a long dining table and chairs in the center of the room polished to a high gleam.

"Is this the *Starling*?" Griffen wondered out loud.

"I'm not sure," Madison said. "The table looks different without all that caviar on it."

The boat seemed to be deserted, so they began to search the cabin. They opened drawers and cabinets, looked under rugs, overturned couch cushions.

Madison began to get frustrated. They didn't have much time. "There's got to be more antiquities here," she said.

"Unless this isn't the *Starling*," Griffen said.

*Maybe it isn't,* Madison thought. Until she remembered something and grinned.

"Did you find something?" Griffen asked.

She crossed the dining room and walked up to the stereo system. She pushed the button she'd bumped into before. Mozart blared from the speakers just as loudly as the night before.

"Ah-ha!" she cried. "That proves this is the same boat!" Alex and Griffen high-fived her.

The three of them raced back to the restaurant. Griffen stopped on the way for a bottle of Pepto Bismol. He even remembered to pour a little out to make it look as though Alex had swallowed some.

Harrison was paying the lunch check as they

entered the dining room and went to their table.

"Sorry we took so long," Alex apologized. "I was blowing major chunks...."

"Please, Alex, spare us the gory details," Judy said. "Are you feeling better?"

"Not really," Alex lied.

"Why don't you go back to the room and rest," Harrison suggested. "Maybe you got too much sun."

Alex kissed his cheek. "Thanks, Dad."

Madison had a feeling they weren't fooling him anymore. But maybe it didn't matter. Maybe Dad trusted them even after all that had happened. That's why they had to find out the truth. No matter what it took.

Alex, Madison, and Griffen hurried to the police station to tell them what they'd discovered. But the police weren't very helpful.

"What do you mean, you won't go to the harbor?" Madison demanded. "We just told you this is the same yacht where we picked up the tackle box."

"The yacht belongs to Mark Saxon," a tall policeman told them. "He's a very powerful man here. We have search and seizure laws in this country just like you do in yours. We cannot board his boat without a reason."

"I'll give you a reason," Madison said. "It's filled with smuggled antiquities!"

"You saw them yourself?" the policeman asked.

"Well, no, not exactly," Alex said.

"I'm sorry," the policeman said. "Without hard evidence, my hands are tied."

Madison, Alex, and Griffen went outside and sat on the station's front steps, trying to figure out what to do next.

"The police won't board the yacht without a good reason," Madison said.

"So we'll give them a good reason," Alex said.

"You have a plan?" Madison asked.

"The best of all plans," Alex replied.

Alex pushed the ignition button and the yacht's engine roared to life. The ship pulled away from the dock—with Alex, Madison, and Griffen at the helm!

Griffen steered the boat out of the slip and into the open water. Alex and Madison danced with excitement on deck.

"Check the rear!" Griffen called to them. "We have company!"

The girls dashed to the stern of the boat and saw four coast guard cutters speeding after them.

"Attention, *Saxon Explorer*," the coast guard

called over a loudspeaker. "Cut your engines."

Alex shrieked. She couldn't believe they were actually doing this! But they had a reason.

"Let them catch us," Alex said. "They'll come aboard and find the evidence and—" She stopped when she saw her sister's face fall. "—and we don't have any evidence."

"Exactly," Madison said. "If we don't find any by the time the coast guard comes aboard—they'll bust us for borrowing this ship!"

The girls frantically began searching for evidence, opening every door and hatch they could find. "They're gaining on us!" Griffen shouted to them.

Alex and Madison ran below deck. *There must be something here somewhere,* Alex thought, tearing the place apart.

"Attention, *Saxon Explorer,*" the coast guard called. "Cut your engines immediately!"

The engine fell silent. "Oh, no!" Madison cried. "Griffen stopped!"

Alex peeked through a porthole, and her knees turned to jelly. The coast guard was charging onto the yacht. "They're coming!" she cried.

# CHAPTER FOURTEEN

"What do we do?" Alex cried, gripping Madison's hand.

"I don't know!" Madison cried back.

Alex and Madison ran from the porthole. A corner of the rug caught hold of Alex's foot and she tripped, slamming right into the wall. *Thump!*

"Are you all right?" Madison asked.

Alex nodded. "Hey," she said. "That wall sounded hollow!"

"It could be a secret hiding place!" Madison exclaimed.

She and Alex quickly started tapping on the wall. Suddenly the wall made an electric whining sound and slid open.

Alex gasped. Behind the wall stood shelves and shelves of precious statues, masks, and pottery.

At that moment the tall policeman charged below deck, followed by a dozen coastguardsmen.

Alex and Madison stood calmly in front of the secret cabinet, smiling.

"You want evidence?" Madison said to the policeman. "We've got evidence."

The Stewart and Grayson families stood outside the police station, waiting for Jordan to be released. Alex was the most anxious of them all.

At last the tall policeman led Jordan out. Alex rushed to hug him.

At that moment, Mark Saxon, the well-dressed owner of the yacht, and Champlaine were led into the station in handcuffs. Alex smiled.

"You should be very proud," the policeman said to the kids' parents. "Your children are heroes."

Madison and Alex hugged their father. He beamed proudly at them. "You know," he said, "I never realized how grown-up you girls are. Maybe you're getting a little old for—"

"Dad?" Alex interrupted. "We were wondering..."

"What?" Harrison asked.

"What are we going to do for winter vacation next year?" Alex replied.

"We hope it's as good as this year's," Madison said. "I mean, this isn't our last family vacation, right?"

That night, Madison stood on the sidelines,

watching everyone dance. The Stewarts and the Graysons had decided to celebrate with a beach party. Everyone was there, and everyone was having fun—even Keegan had found a little boy to play with.

Alex and Jordan were slow dancing, gazing into each other's eyes as if they were in a world of their own. Madison spotted Brianna moving in on them.

*Oh, great,* Madison thought. *Now that witch is going to spoil Alex's perfect moment.*

Madison watched Brianna walk toward them. Then she saw something worse. Scott was heading right for Brianna!

Not watching where he was going, Scott stepped right in front of Brianna. She crashed into him and fell onto the sand.

"Hey, watch it, loser," Brianna snapped.

"Sorry." Scott took her hand and helped her up.

Madison watched as their eyes met.

"On second thought, I should have been watching where *I* was going," Brianna said.

Brianna and Scott stared into each other's eyes as if they'd found their soul mates.

*Scott and Brianna,* Madison thought. *Why didn't I think of that before?*

"I've got to warn you, I'm not very good at this,"

Scott said to Brianna, taking her hand.

"Neither am I," Brianna admitted.

Scott flashed a grin and led her into the crowd of dancers.

Madison checked in on Alex and Jordan. They were so lost in each other's arms, they didn't even notice how close Madison was standing to them.

"I wish this dance could last forever," Alex sighed.

"Don't stop when the music stops," Jordan said.

*Looks like things are peachy there*, Madison thought. Then someone placed a hand on her shoulder. Madison turned and smiled when she saw it was Griffen.

Griffen took her hand. "Hey, don't *I* get some attention?" he asked. He led her to the dance floor, and they swayed to a slow romantic song. Suddenly, Madison reached for Griffen's face and planted a big kiss on his lips.

"What was that for?" Griffen asked.

"Just in case I don't get another chance," Madison replied.

He folded her into his arms. Somehow Madison knew she'd have plenty of chances to kiss him—for a long time to come.

# MARY-KATE & ASHLEY STARRING IN™

Win the *mary-kateandashley* Magazine for a Whole Year Sweepstakes

## OFFICIAL RULES:

1. No purchase necessary.

2. To enter complete the official entry form or hand print your name, address, and phone number along with the words "STARRING IN mary-kateandashley Magazine Sweepstakes" on a 3 x 5 card and mail to: STARRING IN *mary-kateandashley* Magazine Sweepstakes, c/o HarperEntertainment, Attn: Children's Marketing Department, 10 E 53rd Street, New York, NY, 10022. Entries must be received no later than February 1st, 2002. Enter as often as you wish, but each entry must be mailed separately. One entry per envelope. Partially completed, illegible or mechanically reproduced entries will not be accepted. Sponsors are not responsible for lost, late, mutilated, illegible, stolen, postage due, incomplete or misdirected entries. All entries become the property of HarperCollins Publishers, Inc., ("HarperCollins") and will not be returned.

3. Sweepstakes open to all legal residents of the United States (excluding Colorado and Rhode Island), who are between the ages of five and fifteen by February 1st, 2002, excluding employees and immediate family members of HarperCollins, Parachute Properties and Parachute Press, Inc., and their respective subsidiaries and affiliates, officers, directors, shareholders, employees, agents, attorneys, and other representatives (individually and collectively "Parachute"), Dualstar Entertainment Group, Inc., and its subsidiaries and affiliates, officers, directors, shareholders, employees, agents, attorneys, and other representatives (individually and collectively "Dualstar"), H&S Media, and its subsidiaries and affiliates, officers, directors, shareholders, employees, agents, attorneys, and other representatives (individually and collectively "H&S Media"), and their respective parent companies, affiliates, subsidiaries, advertising, promotion and fulfillment agencies, and the persons with whom each of the above are domiciled. Offer void where prohibited or restricted by law.

4. Odds of winning depend on the total number of entries received. Approximately 150,000 sweepstakes notifications published. All prizes will be awarded. Winners will be randomly drawn on or about February 15th, 2002, by HarperCollins, whose decisions are final. Potential winners will be notified by mail and will be required to sign and return an affidavit of eligibility and release of liability within 14 days of notification. Prizes won by minors will be awarded to parent or legal guardian who must sign and return all required legal documents. By acceptance of their prize, winners consent to the use of their names, photographs, likeness, and personal information by HarperCollins, Parachute, Dualstar, and for publicity purposes without further compensation except where prohibited.

5. Twenty five (25) Grand Prize Winners will receive a year's subscription to the *mary-kateandashley* magazine. HarperCollins, Parachute, Dualstar, and H&S Media reserve the right to substitute another prize of equal or of greater value in the event that the winner is unable to receive the prize for any reason. Approximate total retail value: $59.90.

6. Only one prize will be awarded per individual, family, or household. Prizes are non-transferable and cannot be sold or redeemed for cash. No cash substitute is available. Any federal, state, or local taxes are the responsibility of the winner. Sponsor may substitute prize of equal or greater value, if necessary, due to availability.

7. Additional terms: By participating, entrants agree a) to the official rules and decisions of the judges, which will be final in all respects; and to waive any claim to ambiguity of the official rules and b) to release, discharge, hold harmless, and indemnify HarperCollins, Parachute, Dualstar, and their affiliates, subsidiaries, and advertising and promotion agencies from and against any and all liability or damages associated with acceptance, use, or misuse of any prize received in this sweepstakes.

8. Any dispute arising from this Sweepstakes will be determined according to the laws of the State of New York, without reference to its conflict of law principles, and the entrants consent to the personal jurisdiction of the State and Federal courts located in New York County and agree that such courts have exclusive jurisdiction over all such disputes.

9. To obtain the name of the winners, please send your request and a self-addressed stamped envelope (excluding residents of Vermont and Washington) to STARRING IN *mary-kateandashley* Magazine Sweepstakes, c/o HarperEntertainment, 10 East 53rd Street, New York, NY 10022 by March 1st, 2002. Sweepstakes sponsor: HarperCollins Publishers, Inc.